Disney's

My Very First Winnie the Pooh™

Pooh's Puzzling Plant

Adapted by **Agnes Sumner** Illustrated by **Josie Yee**

SCHOLASTIC INC.

New York Toronto London Auckland Sydney
Mexico City New Delhi Hong Kong Buenos Aires

ISBN 0-7172-8964-8

12 11 10 9 8 7 6 5 4 3 2 1   1 2 3 4 5 6/0

Printed in the U.S.A.   56

First Scholastic printing, September 2001

One sunny spring day, Pooh and Christopher Robin found Rabbit working hard in the patch of earth where his garden would eventually grow.

"Hello, Rabbit," said Pooh. "What are you doing with all that dirt?"

"Planting seeds to start my garden," said Rabbit.

"What kind of seeds?" asked Christopher Robin.

"Oh, *all* kinds of seeds," replied Rabbit. "But right now I'm planting pumpkin seeds."

Pooh smiled. "Can a bear of very little brain grow a pumpkin, too?"

"A growing pumpkin needs lots of special care," Rabbit explained. "You must be organized. First, you have to find a good garden spot. Second, you must dig a nice hole for the seed. Third, you have to cover the seed with dirt and pat it down just so. Then it needs plenty of sunshine and water and time to grow."

"That does sound like a lot of work, but I will take good care of it," promised Pooh.

"Well, all right," said Rabbit, handing Pooh a seed.

So Pooh and Christopher Robin went off to find a good garden spot. They found a nice, sunny patch near Pooh's house where it would be perfect to plant the pumpkin seed. Christopher Robin dug a hole for the seed. Then Pooh covered the seed with earth, patting it down just so, the way Rabbit had shown them.

"I will sit here and watch the pumpkin grow," Pooh told Christopher Robin.

"But, Pooh," said Christopher Robin, "the pumpkin won't be ripe until next fall. That's an awful lot of sitting!"

"My pumpkin needs special care," proclaimed Pooh. "And that's just what I will give it, because I promised Rabbit I would."

"Well, a promise is a promise," Christopher Robin remarked.

"But if it's going to take that much sitting, I need to get something to eat," said Pooh. "Is that all right, Christopher Robin?"

"Of course!" answered Christopher Robin.

Pooh went home and soon returned with all of
his honey pots. "I hope this will be enough,"
he thought. "Christopher Robin did say it would
take a lot of sitting."

Then Pooh sat down and he watched the spot
where the seed was planted. He watched and ate.
He ate and watched.

And while he did,
the afternoon turned
into evening. But
there was still no
pumpkin. Finally,
Pooh went home
to sleep.

Early the next morning, Pooh returned to the spot where the seed was planted. Again, he sat and waited . . . and ate. After several weeks of the same sort of thing, it was summer.

"Hello, Pooh," said Piglet one day. "What a pretty vine you're growing!"

"Oh, bother," replied Pooh sadly.

"What's the matter, Pooh?" asked Piglet.

"I wanted a *pumpkin*," Pooh replied.

"Well, it's just beginning, Pooh," said Piglet. "Wait and see. You are taking good care of it. It looks very healthy. Maybe it will surprise you."

So Pooh went on watching, and eating, and caring for the vine.

As summer wore on, a flower appeared. Pooh was looking at the flower, feeling very puzzled, when Owl flew over.

"Good morning, my young friend," said Owl as he landed beside Pooh. "What is this you have here?"

"I'm not sure," said Pooh. "Piglet said it might surprise me, and it has."

After carefully examining the flower, Owl declared, "Pooh, this is an
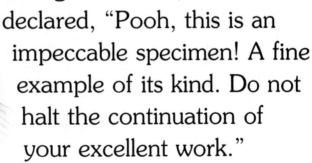
impeccable specimen! A fine example of its kind. Do not halt the continuation of your excellent work."

Pooh looked even more puzzled.

"My dear Pooh, what *is* the matter?" Owl asked.

"Oh, Owl," answered Pooh sadly, "I thought I planted a pumpkin, not a flower!"

"I will be happy to inform you what it is you are growing here," said Owl. "You have a vine. You have a flower. A flower grows on a vine before there is a . . . ah . . . a cucumber! If I am not mistaken, I believe that what you are growing is a fine cucumber."

"Oh, my," Pooh replied. "Do cucumbers taste good with honey?"

Pooh looked back at his plant. It had big leaves and the ends of the vine were curly, like springs. Pooh studied the flower. It was white and shaped sort of like a horn.

"Think, think, think," he said to himself. "Rabbit gave me a *pumpkin* seed. So why would it grow into a cucumber? I'll keep caring for this plant and see what happens. Like Piglet said, it has surprised me. Maybe it will surprise me some more!"

Pooh went back to work, watching the plant and eating his honey.

From time to time, the hot summer sun seemed to dry out the ground. When it did, Pooh got his watering can and watered the plant just like Rabbit had told him.

Occasionally, the sun made Pooh a bit sleepy and he would take a short nap. And in this way, time passed and summer began to turn into autumn.

The air seemed cooler, and the leaves began to change colors, and one day Pooh woke up from a nap and found Eeyore standing over him.

"Pooh, forgive me for mentioning it," Eeyore droned, "but I thought you should know there is a ball of green growing on your vine."

"A ball of green?" Pooh asked.

"Well, look for yourself," replied Eeyore.

"So there is," said Pooh sadly.

"Did you not want a green ball?" Eeyore asked.

"I want a *pumpkin*, Eeyore!" cried Pooh, "not a vine, a flower, a cucumber, *or* a green ball!"

"I've gone this far," thought Pooh to himself. "I might as well just keep watching . . . and eating," Pooh added. "But that's all right, I don't mind. Especially not the eating part!"

The green ball grew . . .

. . . bigger . . .

. . . and bigger.

And as he sat by his plant every day and ate pot after pot of honey, Pooh's tummy grew bigger and bigger, too!

Days and weeks passed.

One morning Pooh saw that a small part of the ball had turned orange. Every day after that it became more and more orange.

Then the air got much cooler and the leaves fell from the trees. And there on Pooh's vine was a huge orange pumpkin!

Everyone gathered around Pooh and his pumpkin. They looked from Pooh to the pumpkin and from the pumpkin back to Pooh.

"That pumpkin's a tiggerific color and it looks just like *your* tummy, Pooh!" laughed Tigger.

"Oh, my! I think you're right," agreed Pooh.

"Silly old bear," said Christopher Robin. "You gave the pumpkin so much care that you grew along with it!"

"Yes, I suppose you might say that honey and pumpkins go very well together!" giggled Pooh.

"Well, then," said Christopher Robin, "how about pumpkin-honey pie? I'm sure Kanga would be happy to make this wonderful pumpkin into a yummy pie for us."

"Super-de-duper-dee-licious!" shouted Tigger, bouncing away toward Kanga's house. Everyone else thought so, too. So off they went, carrying Pooh's extra-special pumpkin!